Dathera Dad

Other Orchard Storybooks

Clipper Street Stories by Bernard Ashley
CALLING FOR SAM
TALLER THAN BEFORE
DOWN–AND–OUT

Folk Tales by Kevin Crossley-Holland
BOO!

Jupiter Jane Stories by Sheila Lavelle
THE APPLE PIE ALIEN
THE BOGGY BAY MARATHON
THE TOPSY–TURVY TEACHER
SPOTS IN SPACE

Woodside School Stories by Jean Ure
THE FRIGHT
WHO'S TALKING?
SOPPY BIRTHDAY

FAIRY TALES

Dathera Dad

Kevin
Crossley-Holland

Illustrated by
Peter Melnyczuk

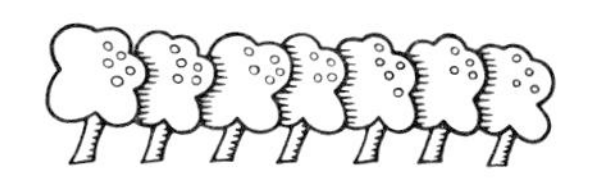

ORCHARD BOOKS
London

First published in Great Britain in 1988 by
ORCHARD BOOKS
10 Golden Square, London W1R 3AF
Orchard Books Australia
14 Mars Road, Lane Cove NSW 2066
Orchard Books Canada
20 Torbay Road, Markham, Ontario 23P 1G6
1 85213 092 X
Typeset in Great Britain by
Tradespools Ltd, Frome, Somerset
Printed in Great Britain by A. Wheaton, Exeter

Contents

The Shepherd's Tale

That's where I saw them! Up on that green patch there . . .

That's fifty years, see. I was missing one ewe and high up and calling. First there was such a winking and glittering. Then I saw them quite clearly—little men and women dancing in a ring.

I'll tell you then. I hurried towards them and first thing caught my eye—they were wearing scarlet or white, every one of them. Scarlet or white. A kind of uniform, see. The men had caps on their heads and the women, they wore white lacy kinds of things. Fantastical! They waved in the wind.

My! Those ladies were lovely! I've seen some beauties, mind, some rare beauties. The men, too, they were handsome.

There were three harpists there, sitting on flat stones and playing for the dancers. Plucking and rippling! The strange thing is I couldn't hear a note. I saw them playing but they didn't make a sound.

Round and round whirled the dancers, smiling and laughing. And when they spied me, they nodded and smiled, and some of them threw up their arms and beckoned me. Then they all joined hands again. Faster and faster, leaning backward,

almost falling! Laughing faces!

There were others, too, mind. Little men running races, sprinting and scurrying, and others clambering over the old cromlech—up one side, along the top, and down the other. That's as old as Adam, that. Prehistorical! Not so long back, two men came all the way from Cardiff just to measure it . . .

Where was I then? Yes, and horses. There were ladies riding

round on dapper white horses. Side-saddle, mind. Their dresses were white—white as misty sunlight and red as young blood.

Well, then, I'll tell you. I came close and very close. I stuck out one foot, just into the ring. I heard it then, the fairy music. Harps, what a sound, yes! My heart started jigging. There's a sound a man could die for.

So I stepped right into the ring, see. At once I saw I was in some kind of palace. The walls were covered with gold and pearls.

One young woman walked up to me. "Come with me, Dai!" That's what she said. "We've been expecting you."

Then she showed me round—all the shining rooms, and the coloured gardens.

"You can go where you want, Dai," she said. "There's just one thing . . ."

"What's that?" I said.

"You see this well?"

I looked into the well and it was teeming with fish, see. Red and blue and black and green. And some of them were gold.

"You see this well?" she said. "Whatever you do, Dai, never drink a drop."

The young woman led me back through the palace to a feasting-hall. There was venison and lamb and sucking-pig; pheasant and grouse and pigeon. All of it carried in on silver platters, mind. And you know who carried it? Beautiful ladies! That was a place, all right!

And there was red wine and yellow wine, I remember that. I drank them both, see. I drank them from gold goblets covered with diamonds and rubies and emeralds. Strong wine and sweet wine! Before then, I'd only tasted water and milk and beer.

Whatever I wanted, they brought it to me. Food, drink, warm water to wash with, a comfortable bed. I wanted harpists, singers, acrobats! Then I wanted to talk to their little children. A whole troop came in, chattering and giggling. They were small as dandelions.

You know what I wanted most? It's always the same, mind. You want what you can't have. That's the old Adam.

After dark, I sneaked out into the garden, see. I ran down to the well.

Then I plunged in this hand—and all the coloured fishes, they disappeared. Then I cupped my hands and lowered them into the water ...

Oh! What a shriek there was! Glassy and piercing, like the moon in pain. A shriek right round the garden and the palace.

Never mind, I closed my eyes and sipped the water!

The garden and the palace and the little people inside it, they all dissolved. In front of my eyes they just dissolved. Mountain mist.

It was dark, hopeless dark, and I was standing alone on the side of the mountain. Up there, that green patch, see. Standing right in the place where I stepped into the ring.

Fairy Ointment

February and freezing. In sunlight and starlight the wind blew from the east. It gripped the land. It poked its fingers under doors and through squints and along passageways.

Joan sat by the fire, and saw faces in it, and journeys and destinations. Joan rubbed her dry lips against each other. Slowly she shook her head.

"An old woman," she said,

"sitting in her bone-house. I grow old dreaming of all the things that never happened."

The wind gave tongue to the elm and the oak, the creaking house, and the taciturn stones: the night was so full of voices that at first

Joan did not hear the knocking at her door.

The noise grew sharper: bare knuckle against wood. Joan stirred. "Of all nights," she said.

She unbolted the door and then the wind swung it wide open and threw in her visitor. He was small and dark like most of the hill-farmers, and he was cross-eyed.

"Well," said Joan, forcing the door back into its frame, "what's blown you in?"

"It's my wife," said the man. "She's gone into labour. Can you come up and help?"

"Up where?" said Joan.

"Up the back," said the man. "Up past the old fishpond. I've brought a horse."

"I see," said Joan.

"That's not her first, mind," said the man.

So Joan parcelled herself inside warm wrappings: gloves and a hood and scarves and leggings and a cloak that was really an old blanket with two holes cut in it for the arms.

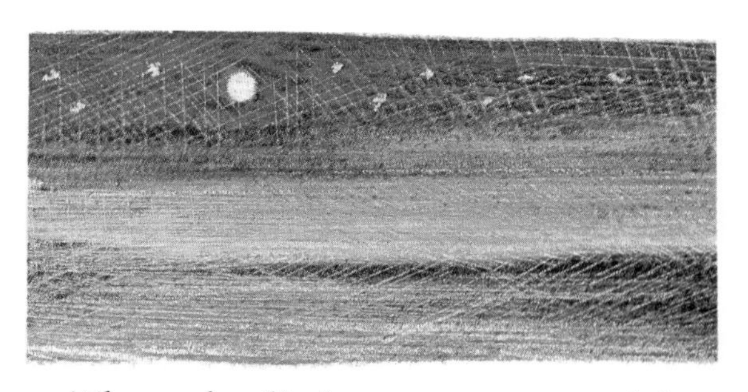

Then the little man mounted his black horse and Joan mounted behind him. The sky's pane was incised with sparkling stars and a full moon; the earth's locked doors were covered with patches of snow. Joan buried her face in her cloak and they rode over the hill at the back, past the blind eye of the fishpond, and up towards the mountain.

No sooner had the little man and Joan galloped into the farm court-yard than a door was thrown open and a young girl ran out calling, "Father! It's a boy! It's a boy!"

Inside the house, Joan was

surrounded by a swarm of children. They followed her out of the big friendly kitchen, chattering and laughing. They followed her down the cold passage and up the stone stairs.

"Shush!" said Joan, rounding on them, and wagging her finger at them. "She can do without that."

The little man led Joan into a hushed bedroom and all the children trooped in after her. The room was lit with candles, at least twenty of them, and the man's wife was lying pale on the bed. Her tiny baby was tucked against her.

"He couldn't wait," said the woman. "The little imp!"

"Now then!" said Joan. Firm and friendly, she pressed her palm against the woman's brow, and plumped her pillows, and then picked up the little baby. He was fast asleep. "Welcome!" said Joan. "Welcome to this wide world!"

The woman raised herself on one elbow and fished in the little cupboard beside her bed. "No need to wake him," she said. "But when he does wake up, will you smear this ointment on his eyelids?"

Joan took the ointment and shook her head. "Whatever you say," she said.

"And be careful," said the little man, "not to get any on your own eyes."

"All right!" said Joan. "Do we

need all these children in here?"

The little man shooed some of his children out of the room, but it didn't seem to do much good. It only made more space for those who were left to wrestle and skip and squabble, and before long, those that went out at the door came in at the window.

Joan washed the baby and still he slept; the little man busied himself downstairs; the woman drowsed after her labour.

Then the baby opened his eyes and Joan saw at once that he had a bit of a squint, just like his father.

"Ah me!" she said, and she shook her head and sighed.

Then Joan picked up the little box of ointment. Anyway, she wondered, what's it for? She opened it, dabbed at it with her little finger, and smeared a little on to each of the baby's eyelids. Then Joan glanced quickly and sideways at the baby's mother, and smeared a little of the ointment on her own right eyelid.

Joan blinked and opened her eyes. With her left she saw no different—the squinting baby on her lap, wound and wrapped in an old white shawl; his sleeping mother in the sagging bedstead; the scruffy children; the simple and homely farm furniture. But with her right eye, Joan saw that she was sitting in an airy and elegant room, surrounded by precious antique

furniture. The baby on her lap was wrapped and wound in gauze flecked with silver and looked more beautiful than before; and his sleeping mother was robed in white silk.

The children in the room, however, looked even less wholesome than they had done before. They were imps with squashed noses and pointed ears. They pulled faces at each other, and scratched their heads like monkeys, and with their hairy paws they picked and plucked their mother's bedclothing, and pulled her ears.

Joan looked and looked. She looked and said nothing.

Before dawn, Joan had finished all her midwife's work. She had washed the baby as clean as a cat's tongue; she had made his mother's bed; she had driven the children out of the room for the seventeenth time; she had put the baby to his mother's breast where he had fed and promptly fallen asleep again. There was nothing more for her to do.

"Take me home now!" Joan said to the little man. She sounded confident enough but she was shaking. She glanced round the beautiful room; she looked at the little man, dressed in velvet, and squinting.

"East, west," she said, "home is best."

Joan needn't have worried. The little man was delighted at the way in which the midwife had looked after his wife and their new baby. He brought his coal-black horse round to the door; and now Joan saw that its eyes were fiery red.

Away they went, into the crystal night, through the burning icy wind. They galloped past the old fishpond, and down to Joan's little cottage at the foot of the hill. There, the little man helped Joan dismount. He thanked her and gave her a gold coin for her night's work. Joan unbolted her door and, safely inside, tested the coin between her teeth. Then she threw some wood on the fire and lay down in front of it. She closed one eye; she closed the other and she fell asleep.

A few days later, Joan picked her way along icy lanes into the nearby town. It was market-day and she needed meat and vegetables; she wanted some company.

In the market, Joan was amongst friends. She had known most of the people there, buyers and sellers alike, for as long as she could remember. So the morning was taken up with a pleasant mixture of business and talk.

While she stood gossiping at one stall, Joan saw something out of the corner of her right eye: a little man, just a couple of feet away, had picked up an apple and, without paying for it, slipped it into his canvas bag.

Joan frowned and watched more carefully as the man sauntered down to the next stall. There, he took two leeks and quickly dropped them into his bag too.

"You!" called Joan. "What do you think you're doing?"

The little dark man whirled round to face her.

"It's you," said Joan, astonished and fearful.

"Good morning, Joan," said the little man.

What Joan had meant to say stayed inside her mouth.

"How's your wife?" she stammered. "The baby?"

"You can see me then?" said the little man.

Joan nodded.

"Which eye, Joan?" asked the little man, smiling.

Joan covered her left eye. She covered her right eye. "This one," she said.

The little dark man raised a hand and lightning flashed in Joan's right eye, a searing dazzle and then shooting stars and then complete darkness.

"That's for meddling!" cried the little man. "That's for taking the ointment, Joan! You won't be seeing me again."

Joan never saw anyone again, not with her right eye. She was blind on that side until the day she died.

The Changeling

Last week there was a wonder.

Up at Hawes's there was a birth, a son to follow four bonny daughters. Such a scowl of a night, but no one was paying any attention to that. There was singing and dancing, all the neighbours in.

They swaddled him in a mesh of
muslin,
They swathed him in pure rainbow
silk . . .

That was the Tuesday, and they arranged with me to baptise the bairn on the Sabbath.

But Saturday morning there was a horrible yelling coming out of the cradle. And when Mrs. Hawes looked in, she saw her bairn had turned yellow and ugly. His nose was a sort of snout, his milkskin had become leathery, and his teeth were already coming through.

Mrs. Hawes cried out, and the farmer and his neighbours, they all rubbed their eyes. It made no difference, of course. The little bairn just lay there and squinted up at them and threshed his legs and yelled.

Poor Mrs. Hawes, she's a fragile woman and she was in a terrible state. When she tried to feed the bairn, he screwed up his eyes, and wrestled around, and groused and grizzled. One way and another, the farmer and his family were unable to get a minute's sleep for the next three nights.

That was when they sent for my lass Janey, and asked her to try her hand. She knows what's what, Janey, just like her mother. She won't stand any nonsense.

Out trooped the farmer and his family, and off to the market. They were all heartily glad to see the back of the little bairn, and to get the sound of that yammering out of their ears.

Janey promised Mrs. Hawes she would be patient. After all . . . the poor wee bairn, it was so ugly and

so sad, and seemed so unhappy with this bright world.

But what with all the weeping and wailing, Janey finally lost her temper. She yelled right back at the bairn, and told him that his mewling was stopping her from winnowing the corn and grinding the meal.

The bairn looked up then and opened its eyes as wide as can be. "Well, Janey," it said clear as clear, with a knowing look. "Well, Janey, loosen the strap! Watch out for your neighbours and I'll work your work."

Then that wee devil climbed out of his cradle. He stretched and grinned and strolled out of the house. He cut the corn, he fed the livestock in the fields; then the wind got up and the mill began to turn . . .

Janey's knees were knocking together. She wasn't going to show it, though. She knew that would only turn bad into worse. So when the wee devil had finished the work and strolled back into the house again, she fed him and played with him until the farmer and his family came home.

As soon as she saw them out of the window, Janey popped the bairn back into the cradle. And at

that, the caterwauling began all over again.

Then Janey took Mrs. Hawes down to the kitchen and told her straight out what had happened. Poor Mrs. Hawes! "What shall I do, Janey? Help me, Janey!"

"The wee devil!" said Janey. "Leave him to me! I'll cook some trouble for him."

At midnight, Janey asked Hawes if he would climb up onto the farmhouse roof and lay three bricks across part of the top of the chimney pot, and she told his wife to work the bellows until the fire was glowing—a bed of red hot coals.

Then my lass, she stripped that wee scrap, she undressed him and threw him on the burning coals.

The little wee fellow shrieked and he screamed.

At once there was a rustling sound, quickly growing, like wind before rain. And then a rattling at the windows and tapping, tapping

at the chimney and banging at the farmhouse doors. That was the fairies, right enough.

"In the name of God," shouted Janey, "bring back the bairn!"

Darkness and wind! The casement window screeched. They brought back the bairn then; they laid him safely in his mother's lap.

And the wee devil? He flew up the chimney laughing.

Monday, Tuesday

Poor Lusmore! He was all misshapen. His legs were bowed, and the hump on his back was as big as a football. When he stood up, he seemed almost to be squatting; and when he sat down, he rested his chin on his knees for support.

Lusmore's arms, though, were strong and tanned, and his fingers were nimble. Almost every day he sat on his low stool outside the cottage where he lived with his old parents—he was almost thirty himself—and plaited rushes and straw into baskets and hats. And he always got a good price for his work because everyone felt so sorry for him.

Everyone talked about him too, of course! Out of his hearing, people said all kinds of things about Lusmore. They said no human being could be as deformed as he was, and that he must be a changeling. They said he warbled strange words to himself. They said he was a master of magic and medicine.

Lusmore seemed unaware of all this. His daily suffering had made him gentle and sweet. He was glad he was alive. He loved birds and butterflies. Every morning in summer, he tucked a foxglove through the band of his straw hat,

and sang as he worked, and eagerly greeted each and every passer-by.

One day, Lusmore rode on the back of a cart into the town of Caher, and sold his baskets and hats in the market there. He did a brisk trade, and went off to drink a few beers afterwards. But when he returned to the deserted market-place, it was late, the light was failing, and the cart and its driver were nowhere to be seen. Poor Lusmore! He had no choice but to walk home.

The little hunchback trudged out of Caher, and by the time he reached the old moat at Knockgrafton it was already quite dark. Lusmore hauled his sad shape of a body off the road and over the molehills and tussocks and sat down on the edge of the old grassy ditch.

"And I'm not halfway home," said Lusmore, and he gave a great sigh—the kind he only permitted himself when no one else was nearby.

The hunchback sat cross-legged,

his chin resting on one knee, and looked at the gibbous moon. Clouds were swarming over it, and it seemed as if the moon were running, or rolling as fast as she could without getting anywhere.

"Like me!" said Lusmore, and he smiled sadly. "Just like me! I'm a poor moon-calf."

Lusmore pressed his chin against his knee and closed his eyes. He listened to the shushing of the light wind in the old lime trees down the road; and then he heard rising above the wind and out of the grassy moat a different sound, clearer and higher in pitch—a song without words. It was the sound of many voices, sweet voices, so mingling and blending that they sounded like one voice. Then the voices began to sing words: "Monday, Tuesday,

Monday, Tuesday, Monday, Tuesday . . ." At this, they paused for a moment, and then they began the melody again.

Lusmore was spellbound by the singing. Though to be sure, he thought to himself, there's not much variety to it. After a while, the hunchback began to hum the melody in tune with the voices; and

then, when they paused, he sang out "Wednesday".

"Monday, Tuesday . . ." sang the voices and Lusmore sang with them, "Monday, Tuesday, Monday, Tuesday . . ." And then, for a second time, "Wednesday".

When the little people heard Lusmore, they were delighted. They skipped and eddied up the bank, and swirled him down to the bottom of the moat in a whirlwind of cries and laughter. The hunchback was twirled round and round, light as a piece of straw, and the fairy fiddlers played faster and faster.

When the world stopped spinning, Lusmore saw he had been swept into a fine fairy pavilion. True, it was rather low ceilinged, but that didn't bother him! The

whole place was lit with candles and packed out with little people—little people chattering, eating, playing fiddles and pipes and harps, dancing . . .

Lusmore was made most welcome: he was given a low stool, and provided with food and drink.

"Grand! I feel grand!" he said as one fairy after another enquired whether he had all he needed, and praised his skill as a singer. “Just grand!” said Lusmore. “I might as well be the king of the whole land!”

Then the music faltered and stopped; the dancers stood still; the feasters put down their knives and forks. Lusmore watched as the little people crowded together in the

middle of the pavilion, and began to whisper. Now the hunchback began to feel nervous: “For all your kindness and courtesy,” he muttered, “you fairy folk, you’re fickle and chancy.”

As Lusmore watched, one little man left the huddle and walked up to him. He smiled at Lusmore and solemnly he said:

"Lusmore! Lusmore!
That hump you wore,
That hump you bore
On your back is no more;
Look down on the floor!
There's your hump, Lusmore!"

As the hunchback looked down, his ugly hump fell from his shoulders and dropped to the ground. Little Lusmore felt so light; he felt so happy; like the cow in the story of the cat and the fiddle, he could have jumped over the moon.

But seeing the hump was scarcely enough! Lusmore raised his arms and clasped the back of his neck.

Then very slowly, for fear of bumping his head against the ceiling, Lusmore lifted his head. For the first time in his life, he stood upright.

Lusmore laughed and then he cried. The fair pavilion, the little people crowding around him, they were all so beautiful. Lusmore began to feel dizzy; his eyesight became dim; he slipped gently to the ground, and fell fast asleep.

When Lusmore woke, the sun was already well up. The dewy grass . . . cows chewing the cud . . . the moat at Knockgrafton . . . Then he remembered! He crossed himself. And still lying on the grass, he reached out with one hand and felt behind his back.

When Lusmore was sure that the hump was not there, he leaped up.

He got down on his knees and said his prayers. Then he saw he was wearing a new suit of clothes, and shook his head, grinning.

So Lusmore stepped out, feeling as light as a piece of thistledown. He had such a spring in his step that you might have thought he had been a dancing-master all his life. His mother and father and all the

people living in the village were astonished at the sight of him—indeed at first glance many of them did not even recognise him. And it wasn't long before the story of how Lusmore had lost his hump was taken to Caher, and then spread for miles and miles around; it was soon the talk of everyone in the midlands of Ireland.

Lusmore had learned to live with his misfortune and now he took his good fortune with a shrug and a smile. Free of his ugly load, he delighted in his dapper appearance, but he had no wish to harum-scarum off to Dublin or climb Croagh Patrick or drink himself into an early grave. He was already in the place he loved, and he was among the friends and neighbours he had known since the day of his birth. He went on with his old job of plaiting rushes and straw.

One morning, Lusmore was sitting in the sunlight outside his cottage door when a woman walked up to him.

"I've come from County Waterford," said the woman. "Over thirty miles. I'm looking for one Lusmore."

"I know him," said Lusmore.

"He had a hump taken off him by the fairies," said the woman. "Is that right?"

"It is," said Lusmore, smiling.

"Well, the son of a neighbour of mine—Jack—Jack Madden the cobbler—he's got a devil of a hump on him. That'll soon be the death of him . . ."

"I am Lusmore," said the little man.

"You!" exclaimed the woman. "Well! There's an omen!"

Lusmore was quite happy to tell the woman what had happened at the old moat at Knockgrafton. He explained about the tune the fairies had sung, and how he had joined in and added to it, and about the fair pavilion, the whispering fairies . . .

The woman thanked Lusmore. She hurried back down the long lanes to her own county. She went straight to her neighbour and it wasn't more than a couple of days before the two of them arranged for a horse and cart to take them and Jack Madden all the way back to Knockgrafton.

On the way there, Jack's mouth was full of complaints. "This jolting," he said. "That'll be the death of me! It's all right for you!" He complained his mother would make him work twice as hard to pay for the cost of the cart. He complained at the taste of the ale they had brought with them. What with his peevishness and the noise of the cart, Jack's mother and her neighbour were worn out by the time they reached the moat at Knockgrafton.

"Don't forget what we've told you," they said. "We'll be back at sunrise." Then the cart rolled away down the road to Caher and Jack Madden was left on his own in the darkness under the rising moon.

Jack hauled his sad shape of a body off the road and over the molehills and tussocks and sat down on the edge of the old grassy ditch. The stillness of the place wrapped itself round him: the clucking of a bird, settling down for the night; a far barking; acres of silence.

And then, out of this silence, from somewhere down in the

moat, rose sweet singing, high-pitched clear singing that made Jack Madden catch his breath and listen intently. The fairies were singing their song just as Lusmore had shaped it for them.

"Monday, Tuesday," they sang, "Monday, Tuesday, Monday, Tuesday, Wednesday." There was no pause in their singing now; the melody and the words were continuous.

Jack Madden's spirit was as shapeless as his body. He had no grace about him, and little sense of the fitting. He listened to the little people sing their song seven times and then, without regard for timing and without thought for pitch, he stood up and bawled out, "WEDNESDAY, THURSDAY".

If one day is good, thought Jack,

two days are better. I should get two suits of clothing!

The fairies whirled up the grassy bank. They lifted Jack off his feet and swept him down to the bottom of the moat and into their pavilion. There they jostled around him, picking at his clothing and banging him with their tiny fists, screeching and screaming "Who spoiled our tune? Who spoiled our tune?"

Then one little man raised his

hand and the crowd of angry fairies fell back. The little man narrowed his eyes at Jack and said:

"Jack Madden! Jack Madden!
Your words were all wrong
For our sweet lovely song.
You're caught in our throng
And your life we will sadden:
Here's two lumps for Jack
Madden."

At this, a troop of twenty of the strongest fairies staggered into the pavilion, carrying Lusmore's hump. They walked over to poor Jack and at once slammed it down on his back, right over his own hump. And as soon as they had done so, it became firmly fixed there, as if it had been nailed down with six-inch nails by the best of carpenters. Then the little people screeched and screamed again, and kicked Jack out of their pavilion into the dark night.

In the morning, Jack Madden's mother and her neighbour came back from Caher. They found Jack lying just outside the moat, with a double hump on his back; he was half-dead.

The two women looked at him; they looked at each other; but for fear of the fairies, they said nothing. They lifted poor Jack and laid him moaning in the bottom of the cart, and rode straight home to Waterford.

What with the terrible weight of his second hump, and the strain of the long jolting journey, Jack Madden didn't live long. "My curse," he muttered just before he died, "my curse on any fool who listens to a fairy tune!"

Dathera Dad

The kitchen was a magic box, full of light and dancing shadows. Shafts of winter sunlight lanced the range and the dresser and the pail of milk, and the hawthorn tree shivered outside the window.

The kettle sang, and the farmer's wife hummed as she put the large saucepan of water on the range, then mixed the ingredients—flour and eggs and breadcrumbs, sugar, salt, suet, then nutmeg and cinnamon and spice.

"And now the brandy," she said, pouring a generous dollop into the mixture, and then a second dollop for good measure.

The farmer's wife put the mixture into a white bowl and covered it with muslin tied round the rim. Then she lowered it into the steaming water.

As soon as the pudding felt the heat of the water, it jumped out of the saucepan. It rolled over the sunlit range and fell on to the floor, cracking the white bowl. It wheeled across the floor towards the farmer's wife.

At that moment there was a loud knock and Tom the tramp put his head round the back door.

"Morning, missus," he said. "Can you spare a pair of shoes?"

"I can't, Tom," said the farmer's wife.

"Christmas, missus."

"Here! You can have this pudding, then," said the farmer's wife, bending down and picking up the pudding in the cracked white bowl. "Christmas pudding!"

Tom was only a few yards down the frosty road when he felt something rolling around in the sack slung over his back. He stopped and opened the sack.

Then the pudding rolled on to the road. The white bowl broke into pieces, and the pudding burst open . . . And out stepped a little fairy child who took one look at Tom the tramp and cried, "Take me home to my dathera dad! Take me home to my dathera dad!"